My BFF's Sister
A Hot Lesbian Romance

The Friends to Lovers Series

by
Reba Bale

MY BFF'S SISTER

© 2021 by Reba Bale

This book is a work of fiction intended for mature audience only. Any resemblance to events, locations, businesses, or actual persons, living or dead, is purely coincidental. All activities depicted occur between consenting characters 18 years or older who are not blood related.

About This Book

Her best friend's sister is strictly off-limits, especially when her friend has no idea that her little sister is a lesbian.

Jewel is back from a long stint in the Peace Corps and ready to start her new life back in her hometown. She's ready to come out to her family and live life without apology.

A chance encounter with her sister's best friend Alice brings back memories of her childhood crush. Alice still sees her as the pesky kid sister, but Jewel is all grown up now and knows exactly how to take what she wants – and she wants Alice.

Can Jewel convince Alice to take a chance on love, even if it may destroy her longest friendship?

"My BFF's Sister" is book two in the "Friends to Lovers" romantic novella series. Each book in the series is a steamy standalone featuring an LGBTQ couple making the leap from friends to lovers.

This book includes explicit sexual activity between consenting adults. It is intended for mature audiences only.

Be sure to check out a free preview of "Spanking Justice: A Middle-Aged Divorcee's First Spanking" at the end of this book!

Want a free book? Join my newsletter and receive a free copy of my book "Hotel Spanking" for free. I promise I will only email you when there are new releases or special sales, so click here[1] and sign up today.

Also by Reba Bale

Affair Recovery
Share Me: A Cheating Husband's Punishment

Dancing with Strangers
Taken by Surprise: A Billionaire Boss Romance

Friends to Lovers
The Divorcee's First Time: A Hot Friends-to-Lovers Lesbian Romance
My BFF's Sister
My Rockstar Assistant
My College Crush
My Fake Girlfriend
My Secret Crush

Paying for Tuition

The Billionaire's Assistant
The Babysitter's Ride Home
The Babysitter's First Ménage
The Teaching Assistant's Lesson

Punishing Holidays
Turkey and a Spanking
Shopping and a Spanking

Sharing With Strangers
The Ride of My Life

Spanking Therapy Clinic
The Reluctant Bride's First Spanking
The Reluctant Bride Gets Caught
The Billionaire Gets Punished
The Curvy Reporter Gets Punished

The Divorce Recovery Team
A Disciplined Budget
Spanking Justice
A Punishing Workout

The Marriage Survival Retreat
Finding His Alpha
Watching His Wife
Exploring His Fantasy

The Voyeur Romance Series
Naughty Dinner Date
Naughty Laundry Day
Naughty Camping
Naughty Love Story
Naughty Sunbathing

Toys for Grown-Ups
Ménage a Geek
Financial Punishment

Unlikely Doms
Alpha in a Sweater Vest
Alpha Student
Alpha Yogi

Standalone

Hotel Spanking
Unlikely Doms
Divorce Recovery Team: A Punishment Experiment Collection
Spicing Up My Marriage
It Takes Three
The Christmas Swap

Table of Contents

Jewel 1
Alice 6
Jewel 10
Alice 15
Jewel 19
Alice 24
Jewel 29
Alice 34
Jewel 39
Epilogue – Alice 42
Special Preview 44
Other Books by Reba Bale 48

Jewel

I walked into the crowded bar, my eyes scanning for my friends. I was meeting several old pals for a "welcome back" party at a local bar that was a popular meeting place. The place was jam packed with young professionals having a few drinks after work.

I was just back from my second tour in the Peace Corps and looking forward to catching up with old friends I hadn't seen in four years. I had loved my time in the Peace Corps, but it was good to be home.

"Jewel!"

I heard my name and waved before heading over to where three of my best friends from college were seated, a pitcher of margaritas already sitting in the middle of the table. After a round of hugs I sat down and grasped the sweaty margarita that was pushed in my direction. I took a sip, my tongue darting out to swipe at the salty rim. I sighed happily. Mmm. It was delicious. I had really missed margaritas while I was in Africa. And bars too, for that matter.

I scanned the clientele and noticed that it was almost exclusively women. "Is this a lesbian bar?" I asked my friends.

"Not technically," my friend Janice replied. "But it's mostly us dykes who hang out here."

I nodded in appreciation as I eyed all the good-looking women who were in here. That was another thing I had missed while I was in Africa—the ability to be open about my sexuality.

Having grown up in in the LGBTQ friendly city of Seattle, it had been a difficult adjustment living in a country where being gay was not only frowned on, but also illegal. My work in the

Peace Corps had been rewarding and I wouldn't have missed it for the world but hiding my true self had been exhausting.

Speaking of hiding my true self...now that I was back in the States, I really needed to come out to my family. I was pretty sure they suspected that I dated women, but my despite my never bringing any boys home we had never really talked about it. My older sister was cool, but my parents were pretty religious.

Even so, it would probably be fine. My sister's best friend had been out since college and my parents treated her like she was a second daughter, so they weren't totally homophobic. But still, I had put off that conversation for as long as I could.

I felt someone staring at me and looked up. The woman looked just like Alice, my older sister's best friend. Our eyes met and held until recognition dawned in the other woman's eyes. Yes, this was definitely Alice. That was weird, I'd just been thinking about her and suddenly she appeared.

I excused myself and walked over to the other table. "Alice? Is that you?"

Alice stood up and pulled me into a warm hug. She smelled good, something citrusy.

"Oh my god Jewel!" she exclaimed. "I heard you were coming back but I didn't expect to run into you here."

Probably because this is a lesbian hangout, I thought wryly.

Alice pulled back and looked at me slowly from head to toe. Her gaze traveled from my well-worn jeans, slung low over my narrow hips, up to my plain black tank, which did nothing to hide my small perky breasts and intricate arm tattoos.

My nipples, unencumbered by a bra, hardened as Alice's gaze lingered there just a moment longer than was acceptable. I felt a rush of arousal, and my nipples poked out to greet her. Alice seemed to shake herself before looking back up to my face with a look of wonder.

"You've really grown up," Alice remarked. "Last time I saw you, you were just a gangly teenager. But now...."

"I'm 26 now," I reminded her. "I've been grown up for a while now."

I'd known Alice almost my whole life. She was best friends with my older sister Maya. They were both seven years older than me and had been friends all through middle school and high school, then they had been roommates in college. I had always been the pesky little sister, trying to follow them around and annoy them.

I knew that Maya and Alice were still good friends, although Maya lived about an hour away from Seattle now. Maya mentioned Alice often when we talked.

Alice looked good, I noted, really good. Her normally wavy brown hair was straightened into a sleek professional curtain. Large brown eyes were bright against her milky white skin. She had large breasts, a trim waist, and a muscular ass.

Yet there was something wild about her. Even in her black pencil skirt and white blouse, something about her screamed Amazon warrior, not boring thirty-three year old aerospace executive.

"I've followed your adventures on your blog," Alice told me. "I love your writing, it's very engaging. I'm glad you had such a great experience in the Peace Corps."

I nodded, feeling pleased at her praise. "It was an incredible experience," I confirmed. "But I was ready to come home to Seattle."

I looked past Alice to the empty table that held a single glass of wine.

"Are you waiting for a date?" I asked.

Alice nodded. "I was supposed to meet someone here, but they just texted to cancel. I was going to finish up my wine and head home."

She nodded towards my friends. "I see you are here with your friends, so I won't keep you. But let me give you my number. Just give me a call if you need anything with your sister not being close anymore."

I programmed Alice's number into my phone, then shot her a quick text to ensure that Alice had my number as well. We stood there awkwardly for a long moment, just looking at each other, and the air around us suddenly felt charged. It was all I could do not to grab Alice and kiss her.

When I was a teen she'd had a huge crush on Alice, even before I fully understood that I was a lesbian. I remembered when Maya told me in passing that Alice had come out to her right after they'd graduated from college. Suddenly those feelings that I'd had for Alice had made more sense. That was the day I accepted that I was also gay.

I had forgotten about the crush until right this minute, when it came rushing back to me with a vengeance. I'd never felt such an immediate and intense attraction to someone before. But it wasn't like I could do anything about it right now.

"Nice to see you Alice," I told her with a smile.

Alice looked almost dazed for a minute.

"Hope to see you soon," I called over my shoulder as I headed back to my friends.

"Who was that?" my friend Janice asked the second I got back to the table.

"Alice. She's my sister's best friend," I responded, carefully keeping my tone neutral.

"She's freaking hot."

I nodded and took a sip of my margarita.

"Yeah no kidding. I had a huge crush on her when I was a kid. I don't think she had any idea though. She was still dating boys then, and I was just the pesky little sister."

Janice smiled. "Well, the way she was looking you up and down, I don't think she's thinking about you like a sister anymore."

I looked at my old friend curiously. "Really? I could have sworn there was a vibe but then I thought maybe I was imagining it. Reliving a childhood crush or something."

"Oh no," Janice answered. "That was definitely an interested look. I know you've been out of the lesbian dating pool for a while, but it'll come back to you now that you're back in the good old U.S.A. That woman wants you."

Alice

I walked into my apartment, my mind completely preoccupied with thoughts of Jewel. And those pert nipples poking through her tight tank top.

What was wrong with me? Ever since I had seen Jewel in that bar I hadn't been able to stop thinking of her. When our eyes had connected I had felt a strong surge of lust, unlike anything I had felt before, strong enough that I'd nearly fell over.

But then I had recognized that it was Jewel. My best friend's baby sister. Someone I had known since she was a toddler chasing after us with a stuffed bear in her hand. That should have been a wet blanket on my attraction, but I was ashamed to say realizing who the hot young woman staring at me was did nothing to dampen my lust.

But Jewel wasn't that little kid trying to annoy us anymore. She was all woman. But it wasn't just that she was Maya's sister. Jewel was also seven years younger than me. I felt like a lecherous old woman lusting after her like that.

I wondered idly if Jewel was a lesbian. Maya had never said anything, so if she was, I was pretty sure she hadn't come out to her family yet. Still, I'd definitely gotten an "interested" vibe from her. Maybe it was wishful thinking, but I could have sworn that Jewel had been checking me out in the restaurant. And her friends had seemed super interested in my when she'd returned to their table, more than a passing interest in who their friend was talking about.

It'd bee a long day. Work had been a nightmare and then the woman I'd met on a dating site had canceled at the last minute, leaving me sitting alone in a bar. And then that meeting with Jewel. I was feeling a bit unsettled.

I dropped my purse by the door and walked quickly towards my bedroom, shedding clothes as I went. Without conscious thought, I eased myself onto my bed and reached into the bedside table for my vibrator. I'd been hoping to get lucky tonight and instead left frustrated. I needed to take the edge off.

I closed my eyes, remembering how Jewel's perky tits pointed out at me from beneath her tight black tank top. I loved it when a woman's breasts fit easily in my palms. I slid my fingers between my slick folds, my breath quickening as I made contact with my sensitive flesh.

It couldn't hurt to fantasize about my friend's little sister, could it? After all, Jewel was technically an adult now, and had been for some time. No one would know.

I turned on the vibrator, slowly moving it up and down my already wet slit, then circling it firmly around my clit. I brought my other had up to pinch my nipple, pulling it long before circling it roughly and pinching it again. I wondered if Jewel liked to have her nipples played with. If she would cry out if I brought those perky nipples between my teeth and bit down.

I closed my eyes and focused the vibrator on my engorged clit, imagining it was Jewel touching me there. My hips rolled against the vibrator, and I moaned loudly, seeking deeper contact. I slid it into my channel, pumping it in and out while I tapped my clit with my fingers.

"Mm, Jewel," I sighed. In my mind's eye I saw Jewel's dark head between my thighs, licking me, gripping my thighs, and bringing me to orgasm with her talented tongue. In my imagination there was no doubt that Jewel was talented at oral.

My orgasm came quickly. My entire body vibrated, and my mouth opened in a silent scream as I rolled on the bed. Slick heat dripped out of me as I came, my hips jerking wildly as I visualized Jewel bringing me to completion. My orgasm seemed to go on forever before I sank into the mattress with a happy sigh.

I waited for the recriminations to hit me as I came down from my orgasm. I knew I should be ashamed of fantasizing about Jewel, but I couldn't bring myself to worry too much.

It had been a long time since I had dated anyone. It was a bummer that my date tonight had canceled. Hopefully we could reschedule. Maybe I just needed to get out there and find myself a relationship. I had been alone too long, that had to be why I'd had such a strong reaction to Jewel.

Yet when I fell into an exhausted sleep, Jewel haunted my dreams. Even still, I was surprised to see a text from Jewel the following day.

Jewel: Hey there. Any chance you're free for dinner tomorrow?

Alice: Sure, I have to work until 6, I could meet you somewhere after.

Jewel: Do you want to go home to change first? I can meet you at your house if you prefer.

Alice: No that's not necessary. If you don't mind coming downtown we can meet near my office.

Jewel: I don't mind. I'm not working right now so I have time.

Alice: Do you like middle eastern food? If yes, how about we meet at Tangier at 6:15?

Jewel: It's a date. I'll wear something cute. (Winking emoji)

I was unaccountably excited by the last text. *Quit being weird,* I scolded myself. *This isn't an actual date. She's a kid. She probably wants advice on finding a job or something.*

Yet when I went to bed that night and fingered myself to orgasm for the second night in a row, it was Jewel's name that fell from my lips.

Jewel

I was waiting for Alice outside of Tangier promptly at 6:15.

Knowing that Alice was coming from work, I'd dressed up a bit, not wanting to embarrass her by showing up in ripped jeans and a tank top. I'd gone with a form-fitting floral dress that stopped a couple of inches above the knee and had a built-in bra that made the most of my modest cleavage. I'd paired the outfit with chunky heels and a bit of make-up to highlight my brown eyes.

I tried not to analyze the fact that I'd spent so much time getting ready for our date. I'd literally thought of nothing else all day.

Alice came rushing up, looking every inch the busy professional in another pencil skirt and blouse combination and sensible black pumps. Today her hair was pulled back in a conservative bun. She looked like every dirty office fantasy I'd ever had. I wanted nothing more than to pull the pins out of her hair and grip it in my fist while I spanked her over a desk. Then I would lick her sweet pussy from behind until she came all over my face.

God, I hoped Alice liked it rough and dirty like I did.

I leaned in to give Alice a hug, purposely pressing my breasts firmly against the older woman and holding the hug a tad bit longer than was necessary. I heard her sharp intake of breath with satisfaction and when we pulled apart, Alice's pupils were wide. Clearly I wasn't the only one affected.

Thank god, because I'd been fantasizing about her non-stop since I'd seen her at the bar.

We were seated at a table in the back corner, thanks to me specifically requesting a private table when I'd made the reservation. I was planning to make my move tonight and I didn't want an audience for our conversation.

"What are you having?" Alice asked we perused the menu. I had a sense that Alice was trying to keep some distance between us.

"How about we share some mezza?" I suggested. I loved the sampler that included a bit of everything and sharing food was incredibly intimate. "And a bottle of wine."

"Sounds good."

We chatted easily while we waited for the food to arrive. I kept the conversation general so that Alice would relax. She seemed a bit tense but loosened up as she told me more about her current job. I shared some stories from my time in the Peace Corps, loving the feeling of making Alice laugh. She had a great smile.

The entire time we talked I could feel the vibration of awareness between us. Every time our gazes would snare the heat between us would ratchet up.

We both reached for a piece of flat bread at the same time, our fingers touching in the middle. Neither of us moved, frozen in place. Alice stared at our hands, her brow wrinkled in confusion, until I moved my hand back.

"I didn't invite you out just to catch up," I began. I waited for her to meet my eyes.

"Oh. Did you want job search advice or something?" Alice asked curiously. I wondered if she was really this clueless about what was happening between us, or if this was all denial.

I put my fork down and leaned in a bit. "I thought I felt a vibe between us the other night," I began. "And my friends thought you were checking me out."

Alice's eyes widened slightly, and she looked a bit panicked. "Um. I don't know what you're talking about."

I kicked off one shoe and stretched my leg out underneath the small table. I ran my foot up the side of Alice's bare leg. Alice gasped, but she didn't pull away. Interesting. Her hand fisted the tablecloth.

"Are you sure you don't know what I'm talking about?" I asked, my voice husky as I looked at her intently. "Cuz I can see your nipples hardening from over here."

"Jewel. What are you doing?" Alice asked. She licked her lips and I felt moisture dampen my panties. The things I wanted to do with those lips...

"What I'm doing is making the first move."

Alice was shaking her head before I finished the sentence. "This really isn't appropriate."

"Why?"

"You're my best friend's little sister."

"So?"

"I'm old enough to be your mother," Alice protested.

Her voice was gradually getting higher as I stroked the skin of her calf with my toes. I laughed and slid my foot up even higher on Alice's leg. "That's bullshit. Not many seven year olds get pregnant Alice. What's your next excuse?"

"I didn't even know you were gay." She was grasping at straws now.

"Now you know that I am. And I'm incredibly attracted to you. I think you feel the same."

My foot traveled above the knee and Alice froze. Our eyes met and held across the table for a long moment. Any lingering doubts that I had about Alice being attracted to me disappeared as the older woman widened her legs beneath the table. I wasn't sure if she'd done it consciously or not, but I scooted forward in my chair and used the opportunity to slide my foot farther up Alice's inner thigh.

Alice's breath was coming in short pants and my own heart was racing like I was running away from a wild animal, which had happened to me more than once when I was in Africa.

"Tell me Alice, if I move my foot another few inches what will I find?"

Alice's legs shifted again, trapping my foot between her firm thighs. I raised my eyebrows and gave her a smile.

"I bet your panties are soaked right now, aren't they Alice? Why don't you open up and let me feel for myself?"

We stared at each other for a long, heated moment before Alice's thighs relaxed open again. I slid my foot up to meet my target, the wet heat between Alice's legs. My toes touched the damp fabric, and I could hear Alice's breath stutter at the contact.

"Soaking wet for me," I whispered as excitement flooded my own core. "You're such a bad girl Alice."

The flare of excitement in Alice's eyes confirmed my suspicion that Alice had submissive tendencies. I tended toward dominant and had developed a pretty good sense for these things. I had dated several women in the past who had high pressure jobs where they had to be in charge all day, and I found that that in the bedroom, they appreciated letting someone else call the shots. Luckily for Alice, I loved to be in charge.

There was nothing in the world like the feeling of an attractive woman trusting me enough to let me have my way with her.

I stroked the crotch of Alice's panties with my foot, pressing against the dampened fabric and running my toes up and down I heard the soft moan of longing that Alice couldn't keep inside. Her eyes were screwed up tight, and her face showed the struggle to keep quiet in the public place.

She looked beautiful and I loved that I was having this affect on her. I was half tempted to duck under the table and make her come before we left, but decided that I wanted our first time to be a little more private. Maybe next time...

"What do you say we get out of here and take this back to your place?" I suggested. I phrased it as a question, but my tone made it sound like an order.

Alice jumped a little, like she was coming out of a trance. She slid her chair back a few inches, until my foot dropped to the floor. I pulled it back and slid my shoe back on.

"I don't think that's a good idea?" she replied, her voice soft and unsure.

"I think it's a great idea. In fact, I think I'm going to tie you to the bed and make you come over and over again until you admit I'm right about what a fantastic idea this is."

Alice gasped, her face flushing red. She looked...intrigued.

I gave her a stern look and purposely made my voice low and commanding. "Now get your sweet ass up and take me home."

Alice

I led the way to my office building a few blocks away, Jewel walking close enough to me that our shoulders brushed with each step. Every touch of our bodies heightened my awareness of her, it was like my skin was on fire beneath the fabric of my blouse.

I couldn't figure out what was wrong with me. I had never had such a strong response to anyone before. When Jewel rubbed her foot on my pussy I'd almost spontaneously combusted. My clit was so swollen right now that it felt almost painful to walk. What was wrong with me?

My car was parked in the underground garage. As we reached my car, I took a deep breath and drew on my logical side. *She's your best friend's sister,* I reminded myself. *Practically a baby.*

She told you she's attracted to you, the devil on my shoulder reminded me. *There's something between you, why not explore it?*

I clicked the key ring, the beeping sounding loud in the almost empty garage, and turned to Jewel. I would tell her that this was a mistake, then I would drive her home and try really hard to never be alone with her again. Or at least until whatever this was between us faded.

"Listen, Jewel, I don't think..."

Before I could finish up my sentence Jewel backed me up against the rear passenger door, trapping me with a hand on either side of my shoulders. The metal felt cool against my overheated back. I gasped, my eyes flying to hers.

"You think too much," Jewel told me. Her voice was strong and confident.

She leaned forward and pressed her lips against mine. They were soft but firm. A jolt of excitement raced through me as Jewel licked at the seam of my lips, demanding entrance. I was powerless to resist.

The second my lips parted, Jewel's tongue swept in, taking control. God, I loved a woman who could take control. So many of the women I dated wanted to do everything by consensus or something. She was so confident, despite her young age. It was a total turn-on.

I gave in to the kiss, relaxing against the car as Jewel moved closer. The kiss was hard and messy and dominant and all consuming. It was the best kiss of my life and in that moment I knew that my life would never be the same again.

Jewel pressed her hips against mine, rolling them against me, and I moaned deep in my throat. Meanwhile the kiss went on and on until I could scarcely remember my own name, let alone all the reasons why this was a terrible idea.

We finally broke apart, chests heaving as we gasped for oxygen. Jewel met my eyes, her gaze hot.

"If you really don't want me Alice, tell me now and I'll go away."

She raised her hand as I opened my mouth to respond, and her voice turned authoritative.

"Don't lie to me though Alice. Because I think you feel this powerful pull between us the same as I do, and that kiss was hot as hell. Tell me, do you want me?"

"I shouldn't," I prevaricated. I was trying desperately to remember why this was such a bad idea. The throbbing in my core was distracting me though.

She raised her eyebrows at me but didn't respond.

"It's wrong." I tried, my voice weak to my own ears.

"That's bullshit." Jewel's retort came fast and furious. "We're both adults. We are old enough to know what we want. And I think you want me as much as I want you. You were already wet at the restaurant. I bet you're soaked through your panties right now."

"I...um..."

"Should I check?" she asked.

I stared at her in confusion. What happened to the little girl who used to follow me and Maya around? Maybe it was from four years in the Peace Corps, but Jewel was grown up and confident in her own skin. She clearly knew what she wanted. And she was right. Whatever this was, it was too powerful to ignore. Maybe it made me weak, but I'd never felt this way about someone before in my life, and I knew I'd always regret not exploring this.

I met Jewel's eyes and took a deep breath to bolster my confidence.

"Come home with me."

Her smile was almost relieved, and I realized that she had as much doubt about my response as I did. "Let's go then."

The ride back to my house was short and quiet. I pulled into the garage of my townhouse and waited for Jewel to follow me into the house. She looked around her, her sharp eyes taking in my modern living room, the art on the wall, and the cluttered dining room table where I often did paperwork.

I dropped my keys and purse on the table by the door then hesitated, suddenly feeling unsure again.

"Do you want something to drink?" I asked, my voice hoarse.

"No. I want something to eat."

"Oh," I answered, surprised at her appetite. We'd had a pretty big meal at Tangier. "Let me look to see what I have. I know I have yogurt and cereal and..."

I paused as Jewel stalked towards me. "No. I want dessert."

Before I could respond she swept all my papers off the dining room table with her arm, sending papers flying in all directions. "What...?"

I stopped as she grabbed my wrist and tugged me near her. "Take off that fucking prissy skirt and get on the table."

Jewel

The look on Alice's face was almost comical. "What?"

"If I have to repeat myself, I'm going to take you over my knee."

Her eyes widened and a flush rose up her cheeks. It didn't take a body language expert to see that my words had turned her on. Her pulse was racing in her throat, and she looked intrigued. I stepped closer.

"Have you ever been spanked, Alice?"

She shook her head, her expression uncertain. I nodded in satisfaction. "Oh good, I'll be your first. Now get your damn skirt off before I rip it off."

Alice reached behind her, the sound of the zipper loud in the quiet of her townhouse. The skirt slowly slid down to her ankles and she stood in front of me wearing her blouse and tiny lace panties in a light shade of pink that almost matched the blush on her beautiful body. She kicked them behind her with one foot as she stared at me.

"Beautiful. Now lose that blouse."

This time she didn't argue. Her fingers fumbled with the buttons before the fabric opened. She shrugged out of the shirt, sending it to the floor on top of the skirt. Her bra was pink and matched the panties.

I gave her a smile as I walked around her, noting with pleasure that the panties were a thong. Damn, I knew she was a wild girl underneath that prim professional exterior.

"Did you wear these for me, baby?" I asked.

She stiffened. "No?" Her voice was uncertain and tinged with embarrassment that told me I was correct. As I stared at her round ass cheeks I couldn't resist giving her a firm slap.

Thwack!

"Ow!" She gasped.

I wrapped my hand around the side of her waist and gave her another smack in the same spot, noting with satisfaction that her pale skin pinked up nicely as the flesh jiggled from the impact.

Thwack!

I gave her a few more firm slaps, alternating between sides.

Thwack!

Thwack!

Thwack!

Thwack!

Alice made a little moaning sound in the back of her throat. I glanced at her face to see her biting her lip.

"Lay on the table," I instructed.

This time she complied without hesitation, sliding her ass onto the heavy wood table, her feet dangling over the edge. I pushed her legs apart and stepped between them, kissing her deeply on the mouth.

She returned my kiss with equal fervor, her hands squeezing my shoulders possessively. I loved seeing her grow bolder. Slowly I broke this kiss and pushed gently until she was laying down flat on her back.

"Bend your knees and rest your feet on the table," I told her.

She scooted her ass back a bit and brought herself into position. I grabbed a chair and moved it so I could sit between her legs. With one hand I reached forward and rubbed my fingers back and forth across the crotch of the panties, like I'd done with my foot in the restaurant.

"Totally soaked," I said in satisfaction. "Just as I predicted. I think that little spanking helped get you hot for me, huh baby?"

Grabbing the waistband of her panties, I slid them over her hips and knees until they wrapped around her ankles. She moved to kick them off, but I stopped her with a hand on her thigh.

"No, I like you restrained."

I could hear her breathing quicken. Leaning over the fabric of her panties, I stared hungrily at her pussy. She was waxed, leaving a landing strip, and her juices were glistening over the pink skin.

"Holy fuck, you're beautiful," I said, hearing the reverence in my voice.

Lowering my head, I licked her from bottom to top, swirling my tongue around her clit before reversing the direction. Alice made a choking sound as I repeated my motion. She grabbed my head, her fingers tightening almost painfully in my hair as she pushed my head where she needed the pressure most.

"You taste incredible," I told her.

I began eating her out like it was my job, paying extra attention to her clit on each pass. When she rolled her hips against my face I grabbed her thighs for leverage and started fucking her weeping hole with my tongue.

"I, Jewel, I need…"

"I know what you need baby," I reassured her.

Changing positions, I shifted one hand to circle her clit roughly while I continued with the tongue fucking. She was close, I could feel her inner muscles starting to quiver against me. I loved how responsive she was.

"Come for me now Alice!" I ordered, giving her clit a hard pinch right before I thrust my tongue inside her as deep as it would go.

"Jewel!" She choked out my name as her body bowed on the table then started spasming wildly. "Jewel!"

I continued stroking her as I lapped up the sweet cream of her release, not stopping until she sagged against the table, boneless.

I leaned back against the chair and watched as she came down, panting. Alice lifted her head and stared at me with a look of shocked confusion. Her hair was askew, tendrils escaping that ridiculous bun.

I reached for her hand, helping her move to standing. Her panties slid to her feet as I reached behind her and unclasped her bra, throwing in on the floor. For a second she looked self-conscious as she stood before me, gloriously naked while I remained fully clothed.

"Where's the bedroom?" I asked.

I thought she might protest, but I was pleased when Alice merely grabbed my hand and led me down the hall to the master bedroom. I looked around the neat and welcoming space, glad to see that she had a wrought iron headboard. I could use that to my advantage.

"Do you have any long scarves?" I asked.

"You want to borrow a scarf?" she asked in confusion.

I chuckled. She might be seven years older than me, but clearly Alice's experience had been pretty vanilla.

"Yes."

She walked to a drawer and opened it. "Take what you want."

I grabbed two long scarves that looked sturdy enough for what I had in mind and moved back towards the bed.

"Get on the bed, baby. On your back, close to the top."

She lay on the navy blue comforter like the best treat I could ever want. I licked my lips, remembering the taste of her in my mouth.

Later, I told myself. I needed to get off before I passed out. I was so turned on I could scarcely function.

I climbed on top of her, straddling her waist and leaning over her torso, then grabbed one hand, bringing it over her head. I looped one scarf around her wrist, wrapping it into a firm knot.

"What are you doing?" she squeaked.

"I told you earlier that I planned to tie you up," I reminded her. Her breath stuttered and I could feel her rubbing her thighs together behind me.

I wrapped the end of the scarf around a metal bar in the headboard, tugging to tighten the knot, then repeated my actions on her other side. With her arms above her head, her breasts perked up to greet me. Her eyes were wide, and her face was flushed with nervousness.

I gave her an encouraging smile. "Now I've got you right where I want you, beautiful."

Alice

I felt like I was in some kind of dirty dream. My best friend's little sister was all grown up, and she'd just tied my wrists to the bedframe after giving me the hottest orgasm of my life. This situation was fucked up on so many levels but right now, I couldn't remember why.

I'd never been tied up before, never had someone spank me. I was shocked at how much it excited me. How had I gotten to be thirty-three and not known it could be like this?

Jewel scooted off the bed and quickly stripped off her clothing. I eagerly took in her slim frame. She had narrow hips and her breasts were on the smaller side, but she was still all woman. Her pussy was bare and glistening. I licked my lips and pulled against my restraints.

As if reading my mind, Jewel came back on the bed, crawling slowly over me until she was bracketing my shoulders with her knees. She shifted and lowered her pussy right over my face.

"Make me come with your tongue," she ordered.

It was a weird juxtaposition: this sweet younger woman with the commanding voice. I had always been an equal partner in all of my romantic relationships and yet, with Jewel, I was finding that giving up control was hot.

I knew instinctively she would never hurt me and frankly, I spent every day being in charge of stuff. It was kind of a relief to lay back and do what I was told, even if I never knew this was what I'd craved.

I licked at Jewel's slit eagerly, smoothing her up and down with my tongue as I heard her breathing quicken above me. Her hips rolled against my face, and I pulled against my restraints, longing to grab onto her hips or pinch those luscious little breasts.

I speared into her with my tongue, as she had done with me, and began to fuck her with my tongue. Jewel and her sweet pussy completely surrounded me, blocking everything else out, and between the restraints and her knees bracketing me, I couldn't move the top half of my body at all. I loved it. Instead of feeling helpless, I felt almost relaxed.

"Yes," Jewel moaned as I continued to lap at her pussy. "Good girl. Keep going."

I felt a flush of pleasure at her words and redoubled my efforts. I could sense Jewel getting close and moved to circle my tongue roughly against her clit, then tapped it a few times.

"Alice!" she gasped.

I sucked the bundle of nerves between my lips and bit down gently, adding suction, until Jewel stilled above me for a moment. Suddenly she came with a long moan, her entire body shaking above me. Her juice was running down my face as she came, and I lapped up as much as I could. She tasted delicious.

When she was finished she rolled over to the side and stretched out next to me, panting as she rested her head on my chest. When she finally caught her breath she looked up and gave me a mischievous smile. "That was fun."

"It was...surprising," I told her honestly.

She shifted to release my hands from the restraints, rubbing my wrists to help bring back the sensation. Her touch was surprisingly tender.

We lay next to each other for a long time, both staring at the ceiling and not talking.

Jewel finally broke the silence. "You liked everything we did?"

I couldn't lie to her. "I've never done things like that, never been tied up or, um, spanked. It was, I mean, it felt really good."

Jewel's smile was satisfied. "What shall we try next, baby? I want to make your dirtiest fantasies come true."

We spent the rest of the night alternating between napping and learning each other's bodies. Jewel was a demanding but tender lover, and I couldn't help but want more of her.

After making each other come over and over again we finally fell into an exhausted sleep. When I woke up the sun was filtering through the window and Jewel was wrapped around my back, one thigh between mine, her hand fingering my pussy.

Seeing that I was awake, she slid two fingers into my channel and pressed her thumb against my clit. Usually, it took me a while to get off with a partner, but Jewel already seemed to know my body as well as I knew my own. She brought me to orgasm quickly and then I rolled over and returned the favor.

"What do you have going on today?" Jewel finally asked as we snuggled afterward.

I peered over at the bedside clock. "Well, I usually go to yoga on Saturday mornings, but I already missed my class," I told her.

"Let's go hiking," she suggested. "We won't have too many more sunny days before the rains start."

I took a quick shower and changed into hiking clothes while Jewel made us a pot of coffee and some breakfast. After we ate some eggs and bacon, I drove her to her place to change and we headed out to a hiking trail outside of the city.

The trails were a bit crowded. Apparently everyone in Seattle had the same idea today. We hiked side by side, sometimes chatting, sometimes just lost in thought as we moved through the trees. We reached the top of a trail that looked out over the mountains, and sat side by side on a rock, lost in thought as we both enjoyed the view.

"I forgot how beautiful it is up here." Jewel finally broke the silence. "I missed the mountains when I was gone."

"What are you planning to do next?" I asked curiously. I recalled her sister telling me that Jewel had spent most of her stint in the Peace Corps working on something related to food.

Jewel drew her knees up to her chest and rested her chin on them. With her hair braided back, her slim frame, and her face fresh and clear of make-up, she could have passed for sixteen instead of twenty-six.

"I'm hoping to do more work on food security," she responded. "That was my specialty in the Peace Corps. In fact, I have an interview with the Seattle Food Bank next week for an educational and outreach position."

"That's great," I responded. "So, you think you'll stay in Seattle now?"

Jewel turned her face to meet my gaze. "This is home," she said simply. "And there's a lot of reasons for me to stay."

We stared at each other for a long time, and I hoped fervently that I was one of her reasons to stay. The thought freaked me the hell out. I'd never been one to jump into a relationship, but even after two days together, the idea of not having Jewel in my life was painful.

I had a sudden flash of insecurity. Was this just a fling for her? Was she just scratching an itch with me, or fulfilling a teenage fantasy? We had agreed to spend today together, but what happened after today?

I was dying to know, but there was no way I was going to be one of those women who initiated a "where is this relationship going?" conversation before enough time had passed. It was amazing to me that my entire future suddenly looked different, based on one night with this woman. I just wasn't sure how she felt. As we made our way back to the car, I wondered how long I should wait to ask how she felt.

Jewel

My phone rang just as I got back to my car in the Seattle Food Bank's parking lot.

"Hello?"

"Jewel, this is your mother."

I smiled as I turned on the car and put her on speaker. Somehow my mother could not understand caller ID. "Yeah mom, I recognize your voice."

"What are you doing?" she asked curiously.

"I just got out of a job interview," I replied. "At the Seattle Food Bank."

"Oh good, I'm glad you're finally going to get a job."

Her tone was dismissive, as usual, and I bristled.

"I've always had a job Mom," I reminded her. "The Peace Corps was a job. A hard one."

She sniffed dismissively. "Hardly."

For some reason my mother was convinced that I'd spent the last four years of my life partying and lounging in the sun instead of working on helping villagers get access to more reliable food resources to avoid famine.

"Was there a reason you called, Mom?" I sighed deeply enough that I knew she'd heard me.

"Yes, your sister is in town this weekend. We're having a family dinner Friday night at seven. We'll see you there."

"Was there a question in there, Mom?" I snipped.

I'd been on my own for a long time, there was no way I was going back to my mother trying to interfere with my life the way she did when I was younger. I hadn't lived in their house since I went away to college eight years ago.

"Jewel, we would love to have you join us for dinner Friday night," my mom said through what sounded like tightly gritted teeth. "Feel free to bring a date if you're seeing anyone."

My mind flashed on Alice. The last week and a half with her had been great. We had quickly fallen into a pattern where I came over to her place after work and spent the night, then we had breakfast together before she headed to work.

During the day I would head to a coffee shop to work on some freelance writing jobs I had picked up, or I would update my blog, which was pretty popular. Then I would go to work out at the gym I'd joined when I gotten back in town. Then I'd spend an hour or two at the place I was staying, usually just long enough to shower and change clothes, before I headed back to Alice's house.

I'd been gone so much that the friends I was staying with temporarily were teasing me that I was the easiest houseguest ever.

Things with Alice were shockingly comfortable. She let me take the lead in the bedroom for the most part, and our lovemaking had been incredibly satisfying. I loved that Alice was up to try anything, and we'd already acted out several of our favorite fantasies.

But it wasn't all sexual. Outside of the bedroom we really enjoyed each other's company, even when we were just cuddling on the couch reading or watching bad TV. We had a lot in common, and yet our interests were varied enough that we weren't bored with each other either.

I knew Alice was still hung up on our age difference and what my sister would say though. She occasionally made remarks about how young I was or my sister freaking out. But I knew my sister would be supportive of us. She was the one person in my life who always was.

A few days later I showed up at my parents' house for family dinner, carrying a cake from a bakery we all liked. No sense in irritating my mother by showing up empty-handed.

"Jewel! My favorite baby sister!"

The minute I entered the house my sister Maya ran over and engulfed me in a long, hard hug. Even though we messaged each other pretty much every day, even when I was in Africa, this was the first time I'd seen her in person in over two years.

"I'm so happy to see your face," I told her.

She gave me a wink and whispered in my ear, "Are you ready for the lecture series? I think Mom's been saving them up for you."

We had both dubbed family dinner "the lecture series" years ago since the bulk of the dinner would entail our mother lecturing one or both of us about whatever she was concerned about that day. Our father usually sat back quietly, his eyes bouncing between us until it was over.

The lectures started pretty quickly. "So Jewel, did you hear about that job yet?" Mom asked as she passed around a large bowl of salad.

"Yeah I have a second interview next week," I told her.

"Oh good, be sure to dress professionally."

Mom continued to give me her tips on interviewing for jobs, despite the fact that she hadn't worked outside the home since she'd gotten pregnant with Maya over thirty years ago. I rolled my eyes at my sister when my mother looked away.

When Mom finally paused to take a breath I interjected, "Yeah Mom, I know how to interview for jobs. I've been employed before."

Mom ignored the snippy response. "Once you get a job maybe you'll find a nice boy and settle down. I'd like to have some grandchildren before I die." S

he shot Maya and I each a reproving glance, letting us both know that our lack of children was deeply disappointing to her.

I took a deep breath and set my fork down. It was time. I had avoided having this conversation with my family long enough. Seattle was a small city. If I didn't come out to them now, it was inevitable they would find out soon enough on their own. I really should have done this in college.

"Actually, speaking of dating, there's something I'd like to tell you," I said, looking around the table. "It's not a big deal but...I'm actually a lesbian."

"Since when?" my mom asked in confusion. "Did you learn that in the Peace Corps?"

Maya interjected before I could. "She's always been a lesbian Mom, she just never told us." My sister met my eyes, her gaze completely accepting. "I was wondering if you would ever come out to us."

"You knew I was gay?" I asked.

Maya nodded.

"It was pretty obvious," my father interjected. I looked over at him in surprise. Maybe Dad wasn't as clueless as I thought.

"Did you all know?" I asked.

"Well, I think your mother was in denial, but yeah I had suspected it for a long time," Dad told me. "The way you never dated boys was a big clue. But I figured you would tell us when you were ready."

I looked over at my mother. Clearly my dad and Maya were OK with this, but Mom was definitely the most conservative of us. She gave me a small smile, and I relaxed a bit. I could almost see her putting the pieces together in her mind.

"OK then, once you get a new job, maybe you'll find a nice woman and settle down," she told me, revising her earlier statement. "And my god, how many times did I have to bring up dating boys before you finally spit that out?"

I laughed, the tension broken.

"Well, actually I am kind of dating someone," I told her. "But it's pretty new."

"You'll bring her to dinner when you're ready then," Mom told me. "And if you like this woman, I'm sure we will too. But she'd better want to have children. I can't wait forever to be a grandmother."

Alice

It felt weird being home alone in the evenings. It had been exactly two weeks since our first date, and I'd already grown accustomed to having Jewel around. The truth was, I was head over heels in love with her.

I told myself I was being ridiculous. That we hadn't been dating long enough. That she was too young. That she was Maya's little sister. That I didn't know how she felt. I reminded myself how I'd always scoffed at those people who claimed they'd fallen in love at first sight.

And yet...it all felt right. I couldn't deny the strength of my emotions. Everything felt so right between us. She might not have said anything yet, but I had no doubt that Jewel was as into this as I was.

The real question was if she was ready to settle down. Because I really wanted to settle down. I wanted to have kids some day and I wasn't getting any younger. I leaned back on the couch and let my imagination wander. In my mind's eye I saw us getting married and having a couple of kids and growing old and gray together.

I just wished I knew if I was being crazy by having these thoughts about Jewel already. I hoped I wasn't misinterpreting the look of love I saw in her eyes.

My musing was interrupted by my phone buzzing with a text. I reached for my phone, wondering if it was Jewel. I wondered how her dinner with her parents was going. She had seemed kind of stressed about it but hadn't really said why. I knew her mother enough to know that she could be a pain in the ass. But it wasn't Jewel, it was her sister.

Maya: You'll never guess what happened at dinner tonight with my parents?

Me: What happened? Your mom went an entire hour without telling you guys how to live your life in a way that was less disappointing to her?

Maya: LOL. No, Jewel finally came out to us. I thought you'd want to know.

Me: ???

Maya: Well you're the one that pointed out all those years ago that she was likely a lesbian. And you were right.

Me: Oh yeah, I remember that. How did your parents react?

Maya: Dad had already figured it out. Mom took it better than I would have expected. It was basically a non-issue with both of them.

Me: Oh, that's good. Coming out is so hard when you don't know if people will support you or not.

Maya: There's more.

Me: What?

Maya: Apparently she's got a girlfriend already. It sounds pretty serious.

Me: Really?

Maya: Yeah, she wants to keep it on the down-low since it's early days, but she seemed pretty happy. Sounds serious.

Me: That's great.

Maya: Listen, I can't hide in the bathroom any longer. I'll hit you up later and we can make plans to get together. I'll tell you the whole story then.

Me: Sounds great. Can't wait to see you!

Jewel knocked on my door about ninety minutes later, looking adorable in a peasant blouse and broomstick skirt. I pulled her in for a quick kiss as I closed the door.

"Hey."

"Hi there," she said, running her lips down my throat. "I know we didn't talk about getting together tonight, but I was hoping you didn't mind."

I laughed and gestured for her to follow me to the kitchen. I poured us each a glass of wine and we settled at the island.

"Jewel, you've been here every night for the last two weeks. It would have been weird if you didn't come over." I took a deep breath and added, "Besides, I really missed you tonight."

She met my eyes. "Things have been going great, haven't they?"

I saw a flash of uncertainty in her eyes, but it passed so quickly I wondered if I'd imagined it. Jewel was normally so confident.

I leaned forward and took her hand in mine. "This has been the best two weeks of my life," I reassured her, my voice sincere. "In fact, I wanted to talk to you about this, because I was hoping we could be exclusive."

She laughed. "I kind of thought we already were. I want that as well, and it's nice to know we are on the same page."

I got up and grabbed her hand, tugging her in the direction of the bedroom. "Let's see what else we're on the same page about."

I woke up the next morning in my favorite place: Jewel's arms. She was a light sleeper, and she woke up as soon as I moved. I glanced over at the clock and gasped.

"Oh my god, it's after ten o'clock!"

I never slept this late and now I'd done in twice in two weeks. Normally Jewel and I were both early risers, but we had stayed up until the wee hours exploring each other's bodies and having so many orgasms that I'd seriously lost count.

I had never been this insatiable in bed before, and it thrilled me that Jewel's appetite seemed to match my own. I rolled over and grimaced as the sheet touched the sensitive skin on my ass. My face heated as I remembered Jewel leaning me over the chair, inserting a bullet vibrator, and spanking my ass until I came so hard I fell over.

Jewel sat up as I got out of bed.

"Ugh, I gotta go, I promised my friends I would go for a run with them today."

"Didn't you get enough exercise last night?" I teased.

I went to the bathroom to pee and brush my teeth, then came out to see Jewel getting dressed in the outfit she'd worn to have dinner with her parents. Last night she'd snuggled in my arms and shared that she'd finally come out to her family. To my surprise she'd even gotten a little bit teary as she recalled how relieved she was that they'd accepted her without question.

I paused to admire her breasts until she covered them with her shirt. Such a shame. "You want some coffee for the road?" I asked.

She kissed my cheek as she walked by to the bathroom. "That would be great baby, thanks."

I met her by the front door a few minutes later with a travel mug of coffee and a smile. "Here you go."

She opened the door, then turned to give me a smile. "See you tonight?" she asked.

I nodded and she leaned in to give me a kiss. I wrapped my arms around her, pulling her close, exploring her mouth with my tongue while she squeezed my tender butt cheeks, making me squirm.

"Oh, Alice, sorry! I didn't realize you had company!"

My best friend's voice filtered through the haze of lust, and we stepped apart just as I heard her continue, "Oh my god, Jewel? Alice? What the fuck?"

Jewel

This wasn't how I wanted my sister to find out about me dating her best friend. I stepped protectively in front of Alice and felt her stiffen behind me. My sister's eyes were fixed over my shoulder, staring at Alice in shock.

"Hey sis," I said lightly, trying to break the tension. "Remember how I told you I was dating someone? Surprise."

Maya gave me a wry look, then turned her gaze back to Alice. "Alice? You're fucking around with my little sister? She's a baby!"

Alice cleared her throat. "Maya, I'm sorry you found out this way, but Jewel is an adult and has been for a while now. And we're not fucking around. Our relationship is new, but it's already pretty serious."

Maya scoffed. "I can't believe you're so desperate that you'd take advantage of my little sister."

"Hey!" I raised my voice and waited for Maya to look my way again. "I don't appreciate the implication there Maya. And not that it's any of your business, but I'm the one who pursued Alice. Dating was my idea. Mine, not hers. I won't have you insulting the woman I love damn it."

"You love her?" Maya asked in surprise.

"You love me?" Alice asked at the same time.

I turned around and wrapped my arms around Alice's waist, then met her beautiful eyes. "I know it's probably too fast and I certainly didn't mean to blurt that out in front of my sister, but yes, I love you Alice."

Alice's eyes filled with tears. "I love you too Jewel."

I raised my eyebrow at her, and she continued, "I thought it would freak you out if I said it too soon, but I love you and I want us to be together for the rest of our lives."

She gave me the sweetest smile and, completely ignoring my sister, lowered her head and gave me a passionate kiss, full of promise. My sister cleared her throat behind us, and we broke apart reluctantly.

"OK well this is weird as shit, but if you guys are happy, you know I'll support you," Maya said. That's what I loved about my sister, she really just rolled with the punches no matter what happened.

"Thanks, that means a lot to me, Maya. And I'm sorry you had to find out like this. What are you doing here anyway?" Alice asked.

"I came to see if my best friend wanted to get brunch," she explained. "I sent you a text but apparently you didn't get it, so I figured you had your phone off."

Alice shook her head, her face turning pink. "No, I haven't checked my phone. We've been kind of, um, busy here."

Maya cringed and put her hand up in a "stop" motion. "Please, for the love of god, don't give me any details."

We both laughed.

"So...brunch?" she asked. "The three of us could go.

"I'm supposed to go for a run with my friends," I reminded her, grabbing my phone. "Let me just text them that I'm not going to make it, then we can all go hang out."

Alice and I wound up spending the rest of the day with my sister, having brunch, and then going to catch a movie they both had been wanting to see. I had been out of the country for so long that I had no idea what any movies were. Alice sat between us, and I held her hand the whole movie. Afterwards we waked around the mall for a while, then headed to a local pub near Alice's house for a couple of drinks.

It was a good day. Our feelings were out in the open now, my sister was on board with our relationship, and the three of us had gotten along well all day, having a lot of fun. I knew that today had taken a lot of pressure off of Alice too.

By the time Maya was on her way back to my parents' house, darkness was falling, and I was dying to be alone with my girlfriend. The minute we got back into Alice's house I grabbed her by the waist and pushed her against the wall. I grabbed her hands, threaded her fingers through mine, and pressed the back of her hands against the wall on either side of her head.

"Say it again," I ordered, making my voice commanding as I stared into her eyes.

Her eyes darked as she replied. "I love you Jewel."

"How long?" I asked.

"Since our first date," she responded without hesitation.

I leaned forward and caught one of her nipples between my teeth, biting down hard enough that she felt it through the fabric of her bra and shirt.

"I should spank you for not telling me earlier."

She groaned as I bit her other nipple, and her hips rolled against mine suggestively. "I hope you do Jewel, I hope you do."

Epilogue – Alice

One year later...

"Are you ready, dear?"

I looked up to see Jewel and Maya's mom standing in the doorway.

"I'm ready."

She led me across the hallway where I would meet my bride. The door opened and Jewel stepped out, looking unbelievably sexy in a short ivory dress that hugged her slim frame, and matching ankle boots with a low heel. Her hair was curled around her face in soft waves, and while she normally didn't wear make-up, today she was wearing mascara and a hint of red at her lips.

"You look beautiful," I told her sincerely.

Her eyes traveled up and down me appreciatively. "You're looking pretty good yourself baby."

I was also wearing ivory, but my dress was a strapless mermaid number that hugged my hips and accented the narrowness of my hourglass shape. I'd put my own hair up in a bun, with soft tendrils framing my face, and Maya had helped me get a perfect smoky eye.

We took each other's hands and stepped out into the sunshine. We'd chosen an outdoor venue, then sweated bullets for months hoping for a dry day. Clearly someone was looking out for us, because the sun was shining, the flowers were blooming, and the air was warm and clear. It was perfect.

Her mom headed back up to her seat in the front, then our wedding march started. Jewel and I walked up the aisle together, smiling all the way. Maya stood in the front, serving as our officiant. She had gotten herself ordained on the internet just for this event.

As I stood before our friends and family and pledged our undying love to each other, I knew that I was the luckiest woman in the world. Over the last year Jewel had become another best friend, and after she'd moved in a few weeks after we'd been outed by Maya, our relationship had just continued to bloom and strengthen. We'd even started talking about having a baby together. I couldn't wait for our life together to move into this next phase.

Maya gave us a smile. "You girls ready to get hitched?" she asked.

Jewel and I turned to each other. "Absolutely."

***

If you liked this book, please consider leave a review on my author page.

Want a free book? Join my newsletter and receive a free copy of my book "Hotel Spanking" for free. Be the first to hear about new releases and sales. Click here[1] and download your free book today.

Be sure to keep reading for a free preview from Reba Bale's "Divorce Recovery" series, available now on all major retailers.

---

1. *https://bit.ly/rebabooks*

Special Preview

Spanking Justice: A Middle-Aged Divorcee's First Spanking
The Divorce Recovery Team Series
Book 1
By Reba Bale

"Congratulations Amy, you're officially divorced."

Mark Winston, her divorce attorney, slid the folder of papers across the heavy wooden desk. Amy leaned forward hesitantly and placed her hand on the folder without picking it up. She could still see a faint tan line where her wedding ring used to be.

She bit her lip and sighed. "Thanks. I guess."

"What is it?" Mark asked, his deep voice causing a shiver down her spine. "Most people are relieved when the process is finally completed. You're free to move forward with your life now, like your ex-husband will do."

Amy nodded. "I know. I hope that feeling of relief will come later. It's just..."

"Just what?" Mark asked, tipping his head to the side curiously.

Amy studied him for a moment. He really was a handsome man. She estimated his age to be early 50s, about ten years older than she was. She had turned forty a few months ago. His hair was dark and thick, with silver highlights near his temples giving him a distinguished air. Small lines bracketed his mouth as he gave her a small encouraging smile. Something about him made her feel comfortable to confide in him.

"I can't help but think about all the things I did wrong in the relationship," she said, her voice small. "If I knew now what I know then, would I have done some things differently to save the relationship."

Mark looked at her intently. "You gave almost twenty years to your marriage Amy. You put your own career on the back burner to raise your son. You kept the house. And then your husband decided to move on to someone younger. It's a pretty typical story, honestly."

"I know," she nodded. "But I've been thinking of all the times I nagged, all the times I was too tired from running around with my son to take care of myself, all the times I said no to sex or date night. John cheated and there's absolutely no excuse for that. But I realize at some point I gave up on the marriage too. I'm having a hard time forgiving myself for the things I did, or didn't do, to keep the relationship alive."

Mark looked at her thoughtfully. "You'll need to forgive yourself in order to move on," he said. "Otherwise, you'll just stagnate and think about the past. You do want to move on, don't you?"

Amy nodded again. "Yes, of course. I just need to stop beating myself up."

Mark steepled his hands on the desk and stared at her intently until she met his gaze for the first time since she walked into the office. His eyes were serious. "What if I told you that we have a way to help you move on? A service that has helped so many women like yourselves recover from their divorces and go on to have a happy life."

She looked at him curiously. "How? What do you mean?"

"Our firm offers a unique service for people like you. People who want to, shall we say, accept the consequences of their own part in the demise of their marriage. We will punish you for your actions, then you can move on. We give you absolution of a sorts. Then you are able to forgive yourself too."

"Punish me? Like what, a spanking?" she laughed, ignoring the small thrill in her belly when she said it.

Mark's eyes sparked as if he knew what she was thinking. "Yes, that's exactly right. We call it our Divorce Discipline package. You agree to be spanked or punished by us for everything you did wrong, then it's over and you can move on."

"You're offering to spank me?" she squeaked.

"That's exactly what I'm offering you. It's safe, confidential and quite therapeutic," he said, pulling an envelope out of his drawer.

"I know it's a lot to think about so take some time. Here's the contract for our Divorce Discipline package. Read it over, and if you decide you want to move forward, call my assistant, and tell her you want a DD appointment with me after hours. I'll handle your case myself."

"Is this a joke?" she asked, looking around for a hidden camera.

For more of the story, check out "Spanking Justice" by Reba Bale, available for immediate download on your favorite retail sites today.

***

Want a free book? Join my newsletter and receive a free copy of my book "Hotel Spanking" for free. I promise I will only email you when there are new releases or special sales, so click here[1] and sign up today.

---

1. *https://bit.ly/rebabooks*

Other Books by Reba Bale

Check out my other books, available on most major online retailers now:

Friends to Lovers Series

The Divorcee's First Time: A Lesbian Romance

My BFF's Sister: A Hot Lesbian Romance

Toys for Grown-Ups Series

Financial Punishment

Menage a Geek

Unlikely Doms Series

Alpha in a Sweater Vest

Alpha Plumber

Hotel Spanking

Alpha Student

Alpha Yogi

Paying for Tuition

The Babysitter's Ride Home

The Babysitter's First Menage

The Teaching Assistant's Lesson

The Voyeur Romance Series

Naughty Sunbathing

Naughty Dinner Date

Naughty Laundry Date

The Spanking Therapy Series

The Reluctant Bride's First Spanking

The Reluctant Bride Gets Caught

The Billionaire Gets Punished

The Curvy Reporter Gets Punished
The Divorce Recovery Series
Spanking Justice: A Middle-Aged Divorcee's First Spanking
A Punishing Workout: Spanked by the Trainer
A Disciplined Budget: Spanked by the Accountant
The Marriage Survival Series
Finding His Alpha: A Wife's First Spanking
Watching His Wife: The First Time Sharing
Exploring His Fantasy: A First Time Gay Ménage
Sharing with Strangers Series
Night Train
The Ride of My Life
Standalones:
Share Me: A Cheating Husband's Punishment

Want a free book? Join my newsletter and receive a free copy of my book "Hotel Spanking" for free. I promise I will only email you when there are new releases or special sales, so click here[1] and sign up today.

About the Author

Reba Bale loves writing naughty stories where the characters are able to tap into their inner fantasies and experience spanking, bondage, humiliation, or other activities on the non-vanilla side of life. When Reba is not writing she is reading the same naughty stories she likes to write.

Be sure to follow Reba on your favorite retailer and sign up for her newsletter so you are first to hear about all the new releases. Click here to join Reba's newsletter mailing list.[2]

---

2.   https://bit.ly/rebabooks

Don't miss out!

Visit the website below and you can sign up to receive emails whenever Reba Bale publishes a new book. There's no charge and no obligation.

https://books2read.com/r/B-A-IDTM-HPWRB

BOOKS 2 READ

Connecting independent readers to independent writers.

Did you love *My BFF's Sister*? Then you should read *The Divorcee's First Time: A Hot Friends-to-Lovers Lesbian Romance*[3] by Reba Bale!

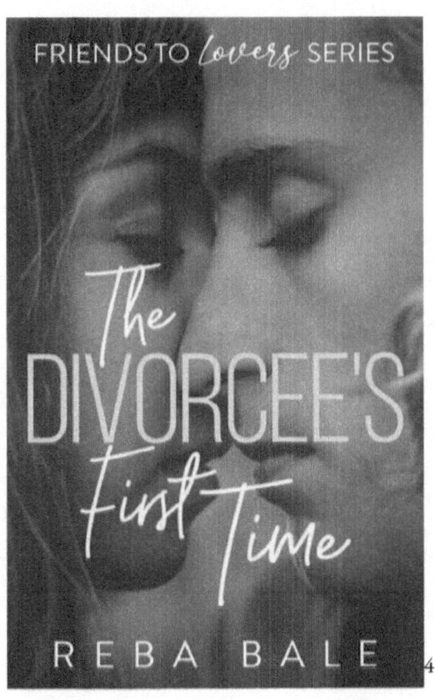

When Jennifer goes out with her best friend Susan to celebrate her divorce, she gets more than she bargained for. The dominant older woman gives Jennifer her first time lesbian experience and changes things forever. Will it be a one-time thing, or will their hot and steamy night lead to more? This friends to lovers novella is standalone romance intended for adult audiences only, due to explicit scenes and light BDSM.

---

3. https://books2read.com/u/bpznKX

4. https://books2read.com/u/bpznKX